W9-AUD-559

JubileeJam®

a not too distant land

By Ellen Love

Written by
ELLEN LOVE

Creative Direction by
ELLEN LOVE

Art Direction & Layout
by **ASHLEY MILLER**
www.aftermidnightdesign.com

Illustrations by
TRACY WAGNER

Jubilee Jam Town Illustrations by
MARK GILES

©2008. All rights reserved.

Second Edition
printed & bound in China
by Jubilee Jam Inc.

Not so far away,
in a not too distant land.
Lies a city on a hill,
known as
JUBILEE JAM.

Adventures for the
BRAVE AT HEART.
Wonders to behold.
Heroes in the making.
Stories still untold.

Treasures on the inside,
transforming in a blink.
Destiny awaits you,
because you are...

**GREATER
THAN YOU THINK.**

**Be sure and look for the
Angel Pies and Handy Heroes shapes
hiding in the cobblestones.**

Hint: There are a total of 42.

Biz-E-Bees
workshop

On any given day, in the
Royal City of Jubilee Jam,
QUEEN NISSI,
the Royal Queen Bee,
can be found overseeing
the making of the Royal Honey –
known as the Royal Jam.

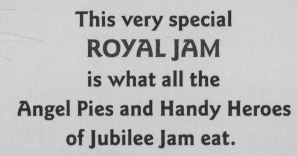

This very special
ROYAL JAM
is what all the
Angel Pies and Handy Heroes
of Jubilee Jam eat.

Royal Jam

The Angel Pies and Handy Heroes
are **ALWAYS** flying off to earth
to place "tiny drops" on
little boys' and girls' foreheads
while they sleep.

This Royal Jam helps boys and girls to be...

JUBILEE GROCERY

STRONGER...

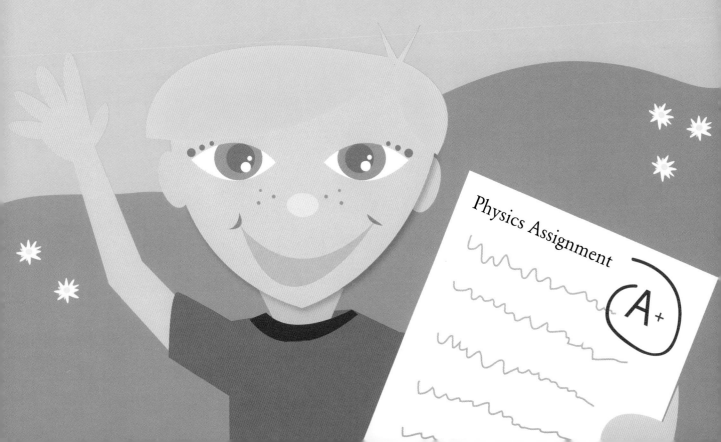

...and **SMARTER**...

Physics Assignment

A+

...and SWEETER...

The Angel Pies and Handy Heroes
even place a "drop or two" on the
MOMS' and **DADS'** foreheads...

Hmm... what am I missing?

Because sometimes, they've forgotten.

1. Be kind to others.
2. Have patience.
3. Love deeply.
4. Keep your word.
5. Be brave.
6. Help those in need.
7. Respect all people.

Whenever the
ROYAL TRUMPET blows
in the Royal City
of Jubilee Jam,
which happens at least
seven royal times a day,
for seven royal minutes…

...a hush falls all throughout the streets, while the Angel Pies and the Handy Heroes gather to hear Queen Nissi announce the **ROYAL ASSIGNMENTS** given by...

...the
ROYAL MAGISTRATE
himself,

For somewhere,
someone needs
a little extra help...
and a little help

GOES A
LOOOOOOOOONG
WAY.

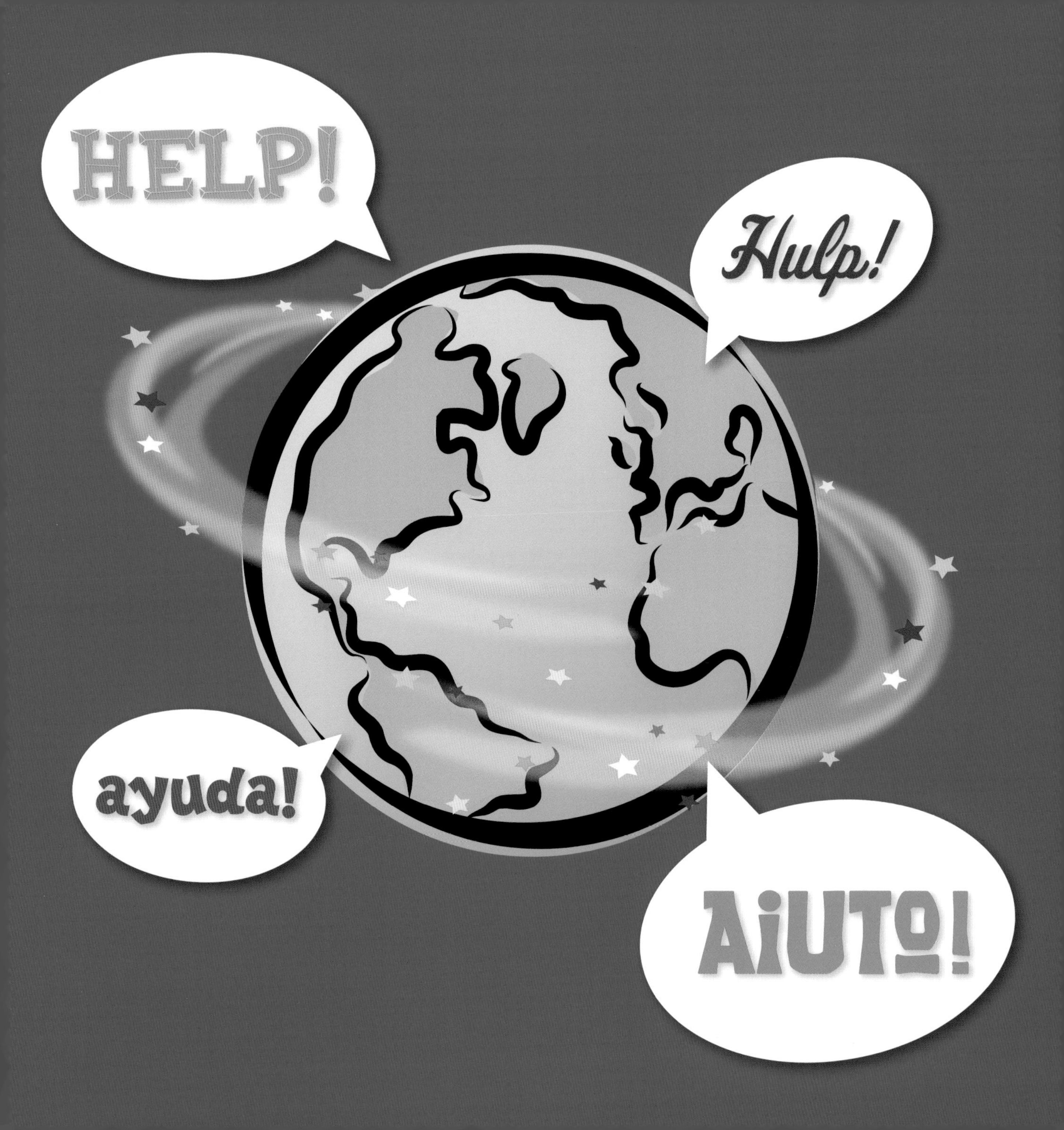
HELP!
Hulp!
ayuda!
AiUTO!

Why just last week,
three of the strongest Handy Heroes
HANDY SANDY, **HANDY ANDY**
and **HANDY DANDY** were sent
to hold up a whole mountain
with their bare hands so it wouldn't
fall under the weight of all that snow
and crush the village below it.

They ate **A LOT** of Royal Jam that day.

And then there was the time
HANDY RANDY, **HANDY GRANDY**,
HANDY LANDY and **BUD** —
the littlest of all the Handy Heroes —
flew off to paint the prettiest sunset you ever saw.

They even took **ROCKY**, the Royal Dog of Jubilee Jam,
who can usually be found raiding the Royal Jam Jar.
That is until Queen Nissi sends the honey bees
to sting his royal tail. No wonder he's always
scratching and chewing in all *those* places.

Royal Jam

Now, don't get me started
on the Angel Pies.
Why, they're just the
cutest things you ever did see.

There's... **PUMKIN,
CUTIE, CHERRY, APPLE,
PUDDIN, PEACHES** and
HANNAH BANANA.
Now Hannah Banana is the
funniest Angel Pie of them all.
She always gets the whole town of
Jubilee Jam roaring with laughter.

Like the time she did
a back flip off a rainbow
and landed right on a big cloud...
Yep, it hailed all over that desert.
The weatherman never
did figure out why.
BUT WE ALL KNEW!

I just love
HANNAH BANANA,
don't you?

Now,
APPLE, **CHERRY**
and **PEACHES**
love to swing on the long swing
hanging from the old, old tree
in the middle of Jubilee Jam.

Once, **PEACHES**
swung all the way 'round
to the cloud shed and
almost knocked over
a whole bucket of rain!
QUEEN NISSI was
NOT very happy about that!

I guess that leaves
CUTIE, PUMKIN and PUDDIN.
They're the oldest of the Angel Pies.

They like to make sure
everybody does just
what they're suppose to
and gets back safe and sound
to Jubilee Jam before the old
Clock Tower strikes SEVEN.

But, it's always seven
in Jubilee Jam
so everything is
ALWAYS on time.
Never early and never late,
everything is **JUST RIGHT!**

YEP, IT'S A FUN PLACE –
JUBILEE JAM,
and we get to go on the
greatest **ADVENTURES** ever!
All of the Angel Pies
and Handy Heroes love to help
boys and girls whenever they need
a little extra help
'cause sometimes they just do.

And their **FAVORITE** assignments of all
are when they get to help boys and girls
find their **LOST TREASURE**.

That's right,
LOST TREASURE!

It's everywhere....
if you know where to
LOOK for it.

Funny thing about lost treasure,
most times you find it
by starting on the **INSIDE**
and before you know it
you've discovered something
you didn't even know was there.....
or maybe you just forgot.

But Angel Pies and Handy Heroes
are right there to remind us.
**THEY ALWAYS KNOW
HOW TO FIND IT.**

So, the next time you
see a rainbow, or a
beautiful pink sunset
or the stars and moon seem
a little extra bright....
that means some
little boy or girl just
found themselves some
LOST TREASURE.

Royal Jam

And we're having ourselves a
ROYAL PARTY in Jubilee Jam!

If you look hard enough,
you might even see
a few **ANGEL PIES**
and **HANDY HEROES**
sliding down a moon beam,
skipping on the mountains or
swinging from a star or two.

So, keep your eyes **OPEN**
'cause you just never
know when you might find
some lost treasure and
where that adventure
might take **YOU!**

ADVENTURE

UNDER CONSTRUCTION

LOST TREASURE

YOUR DESTINY

Jubilee Jam

Good night, good night
from JUBILEE JAM!
We hope you've had fun
and made some new friends.
Come see us again soon.
We'll find new things to do,
And new ways to celebrate
the treasure in
YOU!